Carly
the Schoolfriend Fairy

Special thanks to
Sarah Levison

ORCHARD BOOKS
338 Euston Road, London NW1 3BH
Orchard Books Australia
Level 17/207 Kent Street, Sydney, NSW 2000
A Paperback Original

First published in 2013 by Orchard Books

HiT entertainment

A CIP catalogue record for this book is available
from the British Library.

ISBN 978 1 40832 789 0

1 3 5 7 9 10 8 6 4 2

Printed in Great Britain

The paper and board used in this paperback are natural recyclable
products made from wood grown in sustainable forests. The
manufacturing processes conform to the environmental regulations
of the country of origin.

Orchard Books is a division of Hachette Children's Books,
an Hachette UK company

www.hachette.co.uk

Carly
the Schoolfriend Fairy

by Daisy Meadows

ORCHARD

www.rainbowmagic.co.uk

The Fairyland Palace

Tippingto

Science Museum

Tippington Town

Kirsty's Hotel

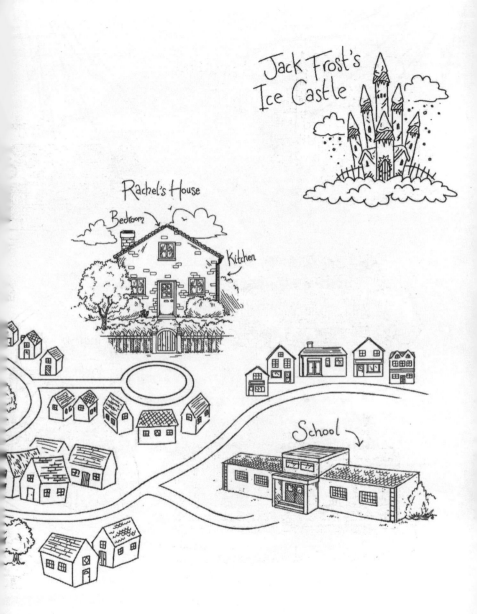

Jack Frost's Ice Castle

Rachel's House

Bedroom

Kitchen

School

My goblins are such a naughty bunch,
Why can't they just behave for once?
Hmm, I know what would be super cool...
I'll send the goblins to human school!

We'll steal Carly's magical objects,
To help the goblins learn new subjects.
My servants will have so much to do,
And I'll get some precious time off, too!

The Spelling Bee

Contents

Competition Countdown

Rachel Walker strolled over to the grand doors of Tippington Town Hall and peered outside. There were minibuses pulling up and lots of people milling around, but no sign of the very special person she was looking for, her best

11

friend, Kirsty Tate!

Rachel's school was taking part in an exciting competition. Four schools from different parts of the country were competing in two different events; a spelling bee was to be held today at Tippington Town Hall and a science contest was to take place at the Science Museum tomorrow. And at the end of the week, there would be a disco at Rachel's school!

Rachel was part of the Tippington School spelling bee team, but the *most* exciting thing was that Kirsty's school, Wetherbury High, was also taking part in the competition. Kirsty was part of the science team and this meant that she was coming to Tippington!

"Rachel! Over here!" called Kirsty.

12

Rachel turned around and there was Kirsty! She was standing with three other children and a friendly-looking teacher.

"There you are! I was wondering when you'd arrive!" said Rachel, running over to Kirsty and giving her a big hug.

Rachel and Kirsty were the very best of friends, and magical things happened whenever they were together! They had met on holiday on Rainspell Island, and since then had enjoyed lots of amazing adventures with the Rainbow Magic fairies. Mean Jack Frost, an icy creature who also lived in Fairyland, was mean to the fairies and always managed to find new ways to upset them. But the girls were always there to help outwit him and his silly goblin servants!

"We came in through the side entrance," said Kirsty with a smile. "This is my teacher, Mrs Richards, and this is the Wetherbury High science team!"

Just then, an official-looking man in a smart suit appeared on the stairs leading up to the auditorium. "Attention please, everyone! I am your spellmaster for today's competition. Will the four teams taking part in the competition please make their way to the backstage area? Members of the audience should take their seats in the auditorium."

"Oooh, not long to go now!" Kirsty smiled, linking arms with Rachel. "Are you nervous?"

"A little bit," admitted Rachel. "But I've been practising my spellings as much as I can! Come and say hello to my team, they're just over here."

15

"So how does a spelling bee competition work?" asked Kirsty, once she'd been introduced to Adam, Amina and Ellie, the rest of the Tippington School team.

Amina explained to Kirsty that the spelling bee was divided into two parts. "First of all there's the 'Spelling Play-Off,' where the teams take it in turns to spell a word," she said. "Then it's the 'Quickfire Challenge', when they have to spell as many words as they can in two minutes. The team with the highest number of points wins!"

"Wow, it sounds very exciting!" said

16

Kirsty with a big smile.

The four spelling bee teams started to make their way to the backstage area.

"I'll join you in a minute!" Rachel called to her team. "I'm just going to walk Kirsty to her seat."

The girls split off from the main group of pupils and teachers in the hall, and made their way towards a side entrance. As they strolled along, something in one of the trophy cabinets caught Kirsty's eye. "Rachel, what *is* that?" she asked, stepping closer.

"It's just the light

17

shining on the Tippington In Bloom cup, isn't it?" replied Rachel, still walking towards the auditorium.

"I think it's something even more special than that!" whispered Kirsty happily, tugging on Rachel's arm. What Rachel saw made her stop suddenly

because there, sitting on the edge of a shiny trophy surrounded by a magical glow, was a beautiful little fairy!

Goblin Thieves

The tiny fairy flew towards the glass door of the cabinet. Rachel and Kirsty gasped, worried that she might fly into the glass, but at the last moment she magically appeared in front of the girls!

"Hello!" the fairy cried, flying a loop-the-loop in the air, "I'm Carly the Schoolfriend Fairy. It's *so* nice to meet you both at last!"

Carly was a very pretty little fairy. She had olive skin and dark hair with a blunt fringe. Her eyes sparkled behind cool glasses. She wore a red tunic with a bright yellow scarf and a white top, and two-tone brogues.

"It's lovely to meet you too, Carly," smiled Kirsty. "Quick, let's hide behind this cabinet before someone spots you!"

The girls and Carly moved behind a large cabinet.

"It's always nice to meet a new fairy friend!" said Rachel, giving the tiny fairy a careful hug. "But why are you here? Is everything OK in Fairyland?"

Carly gave a huge sigh and her sparkly wings drooped. "Oh dear. Something dreadful has happened, and you're really the only ones who can help me!"

Rachel and Kirsty exchanged a worried glance. "We'll do our very best to help," said Kirsty, "but first, please tell us what's gone wrong."

"I think it's easier if I show you," said Carly. She hovered in front of the glass door of the cabinet.

23

She waved her wand and the surface of the glass started to ripple. The girls knew that Carly was creating a Seeing Pool, a magical pool that could show events that had happened in Fairyland!

Carly turned around to face the girls. "You see, I have a *very* important job. My magic makes sure that everyone, both in Fairyland and in your world, enjoys school and learns lots!"

Kirsty and Rachel smiled at Carly.

"That *is* such an important job!" agreed Rachel.

Carly nodded. "Everyone has to go to school, even fairy children. My magical objects help me to look after the most essential areas of school time. My bookbag makes sure that everyone loves words and it helps children to read, write and spell, and to concentrate. My safety goggles make sure that science is lots of fun, and that experiments are safe. And my glitter ball makes sure that everyone enjoys music and special events, like dances and discos!"

The girls looked at the rippling Seeing Pool, where pictures were starting to form. It was like looking at a magical TV! Rachel and Kirsty saw Carly in a classroom, polishing tiny wands. Next to the wands were three glittering objects – a little blue bookbag, a pair of yellow safety goggles and a super-shiny glitter ball.

25

A strange noise came from the scene. *SPLAT!* There it was again!

Carly flew into a classroom next door. The window was open and in the middle of the room were two giant green snowballs. A mouldy leaf with a message was stuck on one of the snowballs. In wobbly handwriting it read: *Ha ha! We tricked you! Silly little fairy!*

"Oh no!" exclaimed Rachel. "This looks like the work of the goblins!"

Carly nodded her head sadly. The Seeing Pool showed the poor little fairy fluttering quickly back to her classroom. But everything was in chaos!

The wands from the cabinet were scattered everywhere and desks were piled on top of each other. And the three magical objects had disappeared!

Carly rushed over to the open window and saw four goblins just reaching the ground. One of the naughty green creatures had the bookbag clutched in his hand, another was wearing the goggles and the glitter ball was being worn as a medallion by a very plump goblin.

"Stop, thieves!" cried Carly.

27

But the goblins pulled faces at her and ran away into the forest.

The Seeing Pool faded.

"I don't understand!" cried Kirsty with a frown. "What do the goblins want with your magical objects?"

"I don't know!" replied Carly, a little tear rolling down her cheek. "But now that they have them, school time everywhere will be in chaos! And it looks like Jack Frost and his naughty goblins are *here*, in Tippington, with my magical bookbag!"

28

"What does that mean?" asked Rachel.

Carly took a shaky breath. "It means that the spelling bee will be ruined. The bookbag looks after reading, writing *and* spelling, and it helps people to concentrate. With the bookbag in the hands of the goblins, the whole competition will be a total disaster!"

Spelling Silliness

An announcement came over the loudspeaker. "The spelling bee will commence in five minutes. All competitors please go to the stage."

"Oh!" cried Rachel. "I have to go!"

"Don't worry, Rachel," said Kirsty, with a determined look on her face. "Join your team. Carly and I will sit in the audience, and keep our eyes open for Jack Frost and his naughty goblins."

31

"Great idea!" agreed Carly, fluttering into Kirsty's pocket. "Good luck, Rachel!"

Rachel headed to the stage. The teams were sitting behind desks on the stage, and a large, heavy curtain shielded them from the audience. Rachel could tell immediately that something was wrong.

Instead of preparing for the competition, Adam was sighing loudly and tearing pages out of his notebook. Amina had her feet up on the desk and was playing her music out loud. Ellie was sitting on the desk, looking absolutely bored.

32

Rachel glanced around the stage to see if there was any sign of the blue bookbag. She noticed that the other teams were also acting very strangely.

The pupils from Wetherbury High were arguing, half of the team from St Martin's were missing, and two of the pupils from Manor College were asleep under their desk!

33

Just then, two judges came onto the stage: a woman with curly grey hair and a short man with a large beard. They were looking rather flustered.

"Where on earth can he *be*?" Rachel overheard the woman judge saying.

"I've no idea," muttered the bearded judge. "We'll have to start without him. It's a good job that we always have a copy of the questions, otherwise the spelling competition would have had to be cancelled!"

"Right, everyone!" called the lady

judge. "It's time to begin. The curtain is about to be pulled back. Everyone in their places, please!"

With a lot of grumbling the teams reluctantly sat behind their desks. A moment later the curtain was pulled back, revealing the audience.

"Welcome to Tippington Town Hall and to the school spelling bee!" said the bearded judge. "We will begin with the 'Spelling Play-Off'. Each team will take it in turn to spell a word from this list." He pulled a piece of paper out from his pocket, but Rachel could see that it was totally blank!

"Oh dear!" mumbled the judge. "Never mind. I know that list like the back of my hand. St Martin's, your word to spell is 'zoo'."

From the audience, Kirsty and Carly could see the St Martin's team looking very confused.

"Is it Z-U-U-U?" replied a small boy with thick curly hair.

"Yes, that is correct. A hundred points to St Martin's!" said the lady judge. "Excellent spelling."

"Oh, no!" whispered Carly, shaking her head crossly. "That *isn't* how you spell 'zoo'! Because my magic bookbag is missing, the teams have forgotten how to spell and the judges don't know either. This is a *disaster*!"

Back on the stage, it was Tippington School's turn. "Your word is very simple," sniffed the lady judge. "It is 'supercalifragilisticexpialidocious'."

"But that isn't a proper word!" cried Rachel.

"No answering back," the judge frowned. "Your team has lost a thousand points. Wetherbury High, you're next."

"That's so unfair!" cried Kirsty from the audience. "Come on, Carly. We have to do something. Let's head straight to the stage!"

Suddenly they heard a commotion.
Then a tall figure strode
onto the stage.
"Here I
am! King
Spellmaster,
ruler of all
who spell and
everyone else
in the whole
world!" cried
the figure, sitting
down on a large,
ornate chair. He
was wearing a suit that
was too short for him and a large cloak,
which looked like it had been made
from one of the stage curtains. Enormous
sunglasses covered most of his face.

As Kirsty and Carly got closer to the stage, Kirsty frowned. "That's funny. He looks different from earlier..."

Carly popped out of Kirsty's pocket for a closer look and gave a loud squeal.

"That's because that *isn't* the spellmaster, it's Jack Frost!"

The Suspicious Spellmaster

Kirsty gasped. Carly was right, Jack Frost was on the stage pretending to be the spellmaster!

"We have to let Rachel know that Jack Frost is here," she whispered to Carly. "Let's creep up the side stairs to the stage."

41

"I'll turn you into a fairy," suggested Carly. "We'll be much smaller and harder to spot." Kirsty glanced around to check that nobody was looking their way. Luckily the lights were low and the audience was chatting and messing about. Kirsty knew that their lack of concentration was a sign that the bookbag wasn't with its rightful fairy owner. They hadn't even noticed that the 'spellmaster' was on stage!

Carly waved her wand and Kirsty felt herself shrinking to the size of a butterfly, with gossamer wings upon her back!

42

"Oh, I *love* being a fairy!" Kirsty whispered, longing to soar up into the air, but knowing that she had to stay out of sight. The two fairies made their way carefully towards the stage, fluttering a few inches above the ground.

"ATTENTION!" Everyone on stage jumped at the spellmaster's loud shout. "I am already BORED of this silly spelling bee. I have decided to make things much more fun. Each team must answer a question about *me*. After all," he smirked, "I am the spellmaster and therefore the most important thing about this competition. The team with the

43

best answer gets a million points. The question is: what is my favourite word? Get thinking!"

Jack Frost sat back on his grand chair, chuckling to himself.

The four spelling bee teams started chatting, but Rachel was staring at the spellmaster in shock. She had just realised it was Jack Frost!

"Pssst! Rachel, over here!" Glancing towards the wings of the stage, Rachel saw Kirsty and Carly behind the curtains. Both fairies were pointing at Jack Frost. Rachel nodded to show them that she knew who he really was. She had to find a way to join Kirsty and Carly so they could work out a plan!

She quickly decided what to do. If her team's answer made Jack Frost angry, he was bound to disqualify them! Even though Rachel wanted her school to do well in the spelling bee, the most important thing was to return Carly's bookbag so that the competition would be fair.

"I think I know what the spellmaster's favourite word is," she said to her team, whispering the word into their ears.

45

"Fine." Ellie shrugged.

"Whatever!" muttered Adam.

Rachel sighed. She was really impatient for Carly's bookbag to be returned to her, then her friends would return to normal, too!

"TIME IS UP!" shouted Jack Frost. "What is my favourite word? *You* may begin!" He strode over to a girl with curly blonde hair and glasses from Manor College.

"Um, we thought it might be 'sunglasses'," stammered the girl. "Yours are very cool and you're wearing them indoors so you obviously like them."

"Hmm," said Jack Frost, stroking his beard with his long, icy fingers. "That isn't my very favourite word but my sunglasses *do* make me look completely fabulous." He spun around and pointed at Rachel's team. "You there! What do *you* think my favourite word is?"

Rachel ducked behind Adam. She didn't want Jack Frost to recognise her! She tried to make her voice a bit deeper than usual.

"Well, sir, we thought it might be..." Rachel paused

47

before saying loudly, "FAIRIES!"

Jack Frost stumbled back in shock, his blue face turning purple with anger. "WHAT! That is the most annoying word EVER! Your team is disqualified! Get out of my sight!"

Rachel and her team quickly left the stage. As they walked past Carly and Kirsty the two fairies fluttered behind

Rachel's hair.

"Well done, Rachel, that was a really clever plan!" whispered Kirsty.

"Thanks, it was quite scary though... Oh!" Rachel almost lost her balance as a gang of 'boys' pushed past her and ran onto the stage.

"Aha, there you are!" Jack Frost said to the four 'boys'. "Everyone, this is the replacement team from Icy Towers!"

The girls peered out at the stage from behind the curtain. They could hardly believe what they saw! Four goblins wearing baseball caps and odd bits of school uniform were standing in front of Jack Frost, and one of them was clutching Carly's blue bookbag!

Tricks and Treats

"Those horrible goblins!" cried Carly, shaking her tiny fist at the stage. "We have to do something and quick!"

"Carly, why don't you make Kirsty human-size again?" said Rachel. "That way we'll be able to move around together more easily."

Carly waved her wand and transformed Kirsty into a girl again. The three friends peered at the stage.

51

Jack Frost was firing spelling challenges at the goblins.

"How do you spell the word 'Tennessee'?" he asked.

"Easy-peasy!" squawked a goblin in an oversized school hat. "T-E-N-N-E-S-S-E-E".

"Excellent!" The lady judge applauded. "Four hundred points to the Icy Towers team. How about 'psychology'?"

"This is soooo simple!" scoffed a goblin wearing a tennis skirt,

spelling the word in super-quick time.

52

"The bookbag is turning the goblins into amazing spellers!" groaned Rachel.

Just then, one of the goblins correctly spelt the word 'gnocchi'. When the goblins learnt that 'gnocchi' was a type of delicious Italian food, they started whingeing about how hungry they were.

"That's it!" declared Kirsty. "The way to get the bookbag from the goblins is to offer them food in exchange. They're so greedy, I'm sure they'll fall for it!"

"Great idea, Kirsty!" cheered Rachel. "But where will we get the food from? And how do we distract Jack Frost? I think he's way too clever to fall for that trick."

"I'll use my fairy magic!" cried Carly. "I'll create some delicious cakes and I'll make Jack Frost's beloved sunglasses fly away! He's bound to try to catch them and then he won't notice what the goblins are up to."

"That's a brilliant plan!" chorused the two girls.

Carly waved her wand and a trolley of delicious-looking cakes appeared. Then the little fairy turned to the stage. She closed her eyes. A moment later, Jack Frost's sunglasses floated off his head!

"What's going on?" screeched the Ice Lord, jumping up to grab the soaring sunnies. He looked like a spidery blue ballet dancer!

54

Carly's magic made the glasses fly all around the stage.

When Jack Frost ran into the audience after his sunglasses, the girls shouted, "Cream cakes! Delicious treats! Come and get them!"

The goblins immediately ran to grab the cakes from the trolley. But Rachel wagged her finger at them. "Wait a moment! You have to give *us* something before *you* can have the cakes," she said with a smile.

"Boooooooooo!" whined the goblins. "We don't have anything to give you!"

55

"Well…" said Kirsty, pretending to think. "How about that blue bookbag?" She pointed at Carly's bag, clutched in the green fingers of one of the goblins.

"Our master said we need to keep this," said the goblin in the tennis skirt, sulkily. "We need to be clever with words so we can go to school."

"But you're AMAZING with words!" Rachel smiled sweetly, wondering why

the goblins wanted to go to school. "I'm sure that silly bookbag doesn't do much at all!"

"She's right," muttered the plump goblin. "We are VERY clever. Let's get rid of the bag. We deserve some treats!"

"Yay!" His chums cheered and the goblin threw the bookbag at Kirsty. The greedy creatures immediately stuffed all the cakes into their mouths.

Kirsty handed the blue bookbag to Carly. It shrank to fairy-size and started to glow magically.

"Oh, thank you!" Carly cried. "I'm going to take this back to Fairyland at once. But I'll see you again very soon!" And, blowing a kiss to the girls, Carly disappeared in a sparkly cloud.

There was a loud howl from the stage.

"You ridiculous creatures!" shouted Jack Frost, who had obviously just discovered the bookbag was missing. "You're never going to win the spelling bee now! We're heading back to the Ice Castle. I want to make sure the other silly fairy items are safe."

The girls heard the goblins and Jack

Frost trudge off the stage and out of the auditorium, squabbling loudly.

All of a sudden the real spellmaster appeared onstage, looking flustered.

"I'm so sorry about the delay," he told the teams and the audience. "I went into a cupboard to fetch a notebook and the door somehow got jammed behind me! Right, let the spelling bee commence!"

Kirsty gave Rachel a big hug and headed into the audience. Everyone settled down quietly.

As the spellmaster asked the first question, Kirsty caught Rachel's eye and the two girls exchanged a secret smile. They knew that now the best team would win fairly. But they still had two of Carly's magical objects to find, and more magical adventures to enjoy!

The Science Contest

Contents

Super Science Museum!

"Bye, Mrs Walker, thanks for the lift!" said Kirsty, hugging Rachel's mum.

"See you later, Mum!" called Rachel, as Mrs Walker got into her car and slowly drove off down the road, waving to the girls.

Kirsty Tate was visiting Tippington with her school, Wetherbury High. Her best friend, Rachel Walker, lived in Tippington and both Kirsty and

65

Rachel's schools were taking part in two exciting competitions! Four schools were competing in a spelling bee and a science contest, and when both events were over, an exciting disco was to be held at Rachel's school.

The previous day the spelling bee had taken place at Tippington Town Hall. The competition had almost been a total disaster thanks to naughty Jack Frost and his goblins. The mean creatures had stolen Carly the Schoolfriend Fairy's three magical objects and, because the objects weren't with their fairy owner, nobody could concentrate properly or learn new things!

Thankfully, the girls had managed to outwit Jack Frost and return the magical bookbag to Carly. The spelling bee eventually went ahead and was won by a school called St Martin's, with Rachel's team a very close second! But there were still two magical objects to find: a pair of safety goggles that made all science experiments in school safe, fun and successful, and a glitter ball that helped make discos, dances and other events fun. Today the science contest was taking place at the Tippington Science Museum.

"It was lovely having breakfast with you this morning," said Kirsty. "And giving Buttons a cuddle!"

"It was so much fun," smiled Rachel,

as the girls walked up the steps of the Science Museum. "And it was very nice of Mrs Richards to give you a lift from the hotel to our house so early this morning! Now, where are you meeting your science team?"

"There they are, by the museum map," replied Kirsty.

"Hello!" called a pretty girl with long blonde hair.

"Hi, Sophia!" said Kirsty. "Hello, Ed and Paul. This is my friend Rachel."

"Hi!" said Rachel, smiling at the others.

68

"Oh, there you are, Kirsty," said Mrs Richards, Kirsty's teacher, joining the group. "I hope you had a lovely morning with Rachel's family. Now, I've just had the schedule given to me." Mrs Richards waved a piece of paper in her hand. "Our science display is due to start in one hour. We're on stand 1D. All the stands are to the side of the main hall between the Space and Flight zones. So, you have forty-five minutes to explore and we'll meet by the stand at 9.45am."

"Great!" cheered the whole Wetherbury High team, excitedly.

69

"Let me show you one of my favourite exhibits," said Rachel. "It's really cool!"

The girls and the rest of the team walked through the museum. There was a huge wheel in the centre of the ground floor. Rachel explained that it was powered by steam, and normally turned round very quickly, but today it was strangely still.

In the Space zone there was an enormous rocket and lots of glowing stars hanging from the ceiling, but as they passed by, the glowing stars faded. The girls exchanged glances. They wondered if the exhibits weren't working properly because Carly's goggles were missing!

"We're going to take a closer look at the rocket," said Ed. "See you back at the stand later!"

"See you soon, we're just going over here!" said Rachel, pointing to a room called 'Light It Up!' that was all about electricity. In the centre of the room were two bicycles connected by leads to a giant light bulb!

"This is *really* fun," said Rachel to Kirsty, jumping on a bike. "If we both pedal quickly, we'll generate enough electricity for the bulb to light up!"

"Brilliant!" cheered Kirsty, hopping on the other bike and starting to pedal.

The two girls pedalled as fast as they could but nothing happened.

"That's really strange," frowned Kirsty.

Suddenly a glow started to come from the light bulb. But it looked like a very *magical* glow!

Cool Rainforest!

The girls watched the glow becoming brighter and brighter until they had to close their eyes. They heard a *POP!* and a tiny voice said, "Good morning, girls!"

They opened their eyes and there, hovering in front of the bikes, was Carly the Schoolfriend Fairy!

"Hello, Carly," smiled Rachel.

75

"It was very clever of you to appear near the light bulb!"

Their fairy friend gave a small sigh. "Because my magical safety goggles are missing, you could have pedalled all day and you *still* wouldn't have made the bulb light up! Until I get my  goggles back, no experiments will work properly. And I'm afraid that also includes all the school science contest experiments."

Kirsty frowned. "We noticed that some of the other exhibits aren't working either. We *have* to find your goggles!"

"Yes," agreed Carly. "The good news is that my safety goggles are here, in the museum. The bad news is that they are being guarded by five goblins."

"The museum is very big," said Rachel, thinking of all the different places where the goblins could hide. "Let's split up to look around properly. I know the museum really well so you two should stick together and I can whizz around quickly."

"Good plan," nodded Kirsty.

The three friends exchanged a quick hug and Carly fluttered into the top of Kirsty's backpack.

Kirsty hurried towards the Space section and Rachel headed into the Eco zone, which was at the back of the building.

The front part of the Eco zone was a mini rainforest, with lots of exotic plants, flowers and butterflies. It was always really hot and humid in there. But as Rachel went into the section, she shivered. It was freezing cold! The exotic plants and flowers were drooping and the butterflies looked very sad. Two children, who were monitoring moisture in the air with a special machine, looked worried.

Rachel knew that the zone wasn't working properly because Carly's goggles were missing! She left the chilly rainforest and went into the Garden section.

As she went through the swing doors, she heard a loud screech and a cry of "Shan't!" coming from the back of the garden, near a big muddy flowerbed.

"Aha!" cried Rachel, "Goblins!" She crept over to the flowerbed. As she got closer, she could see several small people playing in the mud with spades, wearing overalls and caps. But, as one of the small figures turned around, Rachel saw that it was a muddy little boy, not a muddy green goblin!

As Rachel headed out of the Eco zone, a strange announcement came over the loudspeaker.

"HELLO! We are now doing 'The Best Experiment Ever' with some cool chemicals, and... *OW!* Get your silly green hands off *my* special goggles!" There was the sound of squabbling and then a loud screech, followed by silence.

"That must be the goblins!" Rachel thought, and she started to run towards the stalls that had been set up for the school experiments in the

80

main hall.

As Rachel ran into the hall, almost bumping into Kirsty, they heard the sound of clapping coming from a large group of children nearby, who were gathered in front of a display area. The girls quickly pushed their way to the front of the group. In the display area they saw four green goblins!

Snowy Scientists

Rachel and Kirsty watched as the goblins pranced around the display area, enjoying all the attention they were getting from the crowd of children.

The green creatures were wearing very long lab coats that they kept tripping over. Long gloves covered their hands and arms, and each goblin was wearing a pair of safety goggles.

"Carly!" whispered Rachel, peering into the top of Kirsty's bag. "They're *all* wearing safety goggles! Which ones are yours?"

Carly peeped out of the bag. "I don't think any of them are," she replied. "Mine are a gorgeous golden colour. But if you help me out, I'll take a closer look."

Kirsty took off her backpack and put it on the floor. Rachel bent down and carefully lifted Carly out of the pocket. The little fairy flew under Rachel's hair and the three friends made their way to the front of the group.

In the display area one of the goblins was holding up a huge basin of water. Another goblin had a very large test tube clutched in both hands, full of white granules.

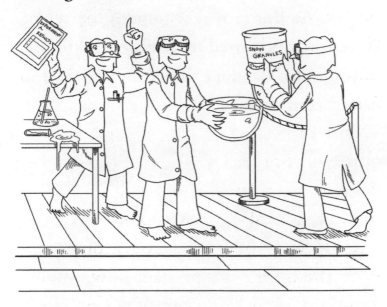

"We will now show you silly lot how to make snow!" shouted a bossy goblin with two warts on his nose. He was holding a clipboard. "Lovely, fluffy snow! Right lads, pour just a few granules into the water. Oh!"

The goblin with the test tube had emptied all of the white granules into the water. As the crowd watched, the water in the basin started to bubble and foam. The goblin holding the basin shrieked in terror and dropped it on the floor.

The warty goblin promptly slipped over, grabbing hold of another goblin on his way down and making him fall over, too! Within seconds all four goblins were on the floor, slipping and sliding on the gooey, sticky snow. The crowd thought that this was all part of the show and applauded as the goblins squabbled and threw handfuls of gooey stuff at each other.

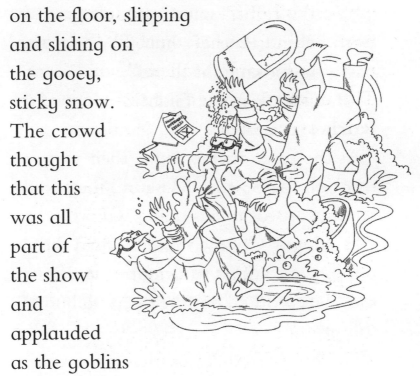

87

"Oh dear," sighed Kirsty. "What a mess! Your magic safety goggles can't be here, Carly, or the experiment would have gone really well."

"You're right," said Carly, peeping out from behind Rachel's hair. "We'd better carry on looking for them."

"Let's look in the Flight zone next," Rachel suggested.

As the three friends made their way through the Science Museum, they could see all sorts of things going wrong.

In Manor College's display area the pupils were trying to demonstrate how magnets worked but they kept falling to the ground!

Rachel waved at her friends from the Tippington School science team, who were looking very sad. She could see that the balloons they were trying to blow up for their balloon rocket experiment had big holes in, and that the nose cone had fallen off the rocket.

"Look out!" cried a voice suddenly as the girls walked into the Flight zone. A model aeroplane swooped down close to the girls' heads, forcing them to duck!

"Sorry!" called a young boy, running past them with the plane controls in his hand. "The plane seems to have a mind of its own today!"

"It must be hard to control because your goggles are missing," said Kirsty, turning to look at Carly. But both

Rachel and Carly were staring up at the ceiling of the Science Museum. Kirsty followed their gaze and there, dangling from the window of a *real* fighter plane hung from the ceiling, were Carly's magical goggles!

Flying High

"Hurrah! We've found the goggles!" cheered Kirsty. She looked up at the plane again. It was a long way up. "But how do we get them back?"

Carly, who was fluttering up and down in excitement, paused. "Perhaps I could fly up," she said thoughtfully. "But I'm worried about being hit by one of those big model planes."

"Why don't you turn us into fairies too?" Rachel suggested. "That way we can work as a fairy team!"

"That's a brilliant idea," agreed Carly. The three friends headed to a quiet corner. Carly waved her wand and a trail of fairy sparkles surrounded Kirsty and Rachel. The two friends held hands as they felt themselves shrinking to fairy-size. It was the best feeling in the world!

The three fairies looked up at the goggles.

"We're going to have to be *very* careful up there," said Rachel thoughtfully. "There are lots of aeroplanes flying around."

"I've got an idea!" said Kirsty, as she looked at the small planes flying through the air. "Why don't we use a model plane to reach the goggles? We're just the right size to fit in one!"

"Great plan, Kirsty!" cheered Carly. "I'll use my fairy magic to fly the plane. We can go right past the goggles and grab them!"

95

The three friends carefully made their way to the model planes. There were quite a few people around but luckily they were very busy trying to control the low-flying planes! The fairies quickly hopped into a dark blue model plane and Carly waved her wand. The propeller started to turn and seconds later they were off!

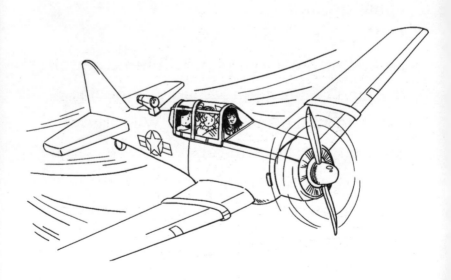

In no time at all they were up in the air by the fighter plane. But as they swooped closer to the window, they got a shock: in the cockpit there was a naughty goblin!

"Oh no!" cried Kirsty. "That goblin is guarding your goggles, Carly. If we get close enough to grab the goggles, he'll be able to grab *us*!"

Carly landed the model plane on top of the real plane and the three friends carefully climbed out. As they peered over the side they gulped. They were a long way up. Rachel and Kirsty were very glad they had wings!

"What's that strange noise?" asked Rachel. The friends listened. There was a glugging, squelching noise coming from inside the goblin's plane, like water going down a drain.

"Oooooooooh! Poor me! Why do *I* have to guard the silly goggles? It's so high up! I'm so scared!"

The girls realised it was the goblin, snivelling and sobbing!

"I wonder how we can trick the goblin into giving us the goggles," said Kirsty thoughtfully.

"I know!" squealed Carly. "If I use my magic to make him small and give him wings, he'll be able to join his friends down on the ground and we can get the magical goggles!"

"Let's try it!" said Kirsty, and the friends fluttered over to the plane's window. It was time to trick the goblin!

A Plane and a Plan!

The goblin spotted the three friends and opened the window.

"What do *you* want?" he scowled.

"Oooooh, we're having a lovely time flying around!" Rachel said, flying a figure of eight in the air. "We can go wherever we like!"

"Don't rub it in," sniffed the goblin.

"Jack Frost used his magic to put me up here so I could look after the silly goggles. But I've been stuck here in this horrid plane for *ages*. And I'm scared, cold and hungry!"

"Poor you," said Kirsty, "and all your friends are having so much fun down on the ground!"

"I'd do anything to get down," said the goblin wistfully, peering out of the plane window at the ground far below.

"Well," said Carly, pretending to think hard. "You've done such a good job of looking after the goggles that I'm sure Jack Frost would want you to go and join your  friends. After all, the goggles can't go anywhere! I'm too little to carry them down to the ground. Why don't I help you to get down and *we'll* look after the goggles up here?"

Kirsty and Rachel gave each other a small smile. Clever Carly was telling the truth! She couldn't carry the goggles down to the ground by herself when they

103

were big, but with the goblin out of the way she could use her magic to shrink them to fairy-size!

"Hmmm," said the goblin, thinking hard. "I guess so. After all, you pesky fairies are the size of fleas so what harm could you do?"

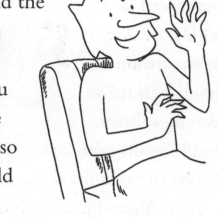

Carly frowned. What a rude goblin!

"I'm going to make you small and give you wings," she said. "The magic won't last for very long so you must fly straight down to the ground."

Carly waved her wand and the goblin shrank to fairy-size, complete with leathery green wings! He looked very scared. Kirsty felt sorry for him so she took his hand and flew with him down to the ground, being careful to stay close to the wall out of sight *and*

out of the way of the model planes.

They landed just behind the glider and immediately the goblin became his normal size again. He was so happy to have his feet on the ground that he immediately ran off to find his friends. It seemed he had forgotten all about Carly's goggles!

A moment later the blue model plane landed and Rachel and Carly climbed

out. The goggles were now fairy-size!
Carly turned Kirsty and Rachel back to
their normal size.

"Thank you,
girls!" she smiled.
"It's time for
me to return
the magical
goggles to
Fairyland
and it's time
for your science
display, Kirsty!" She
blew a kiss to the girls and disappeared
in a glittering cloud.

The two friends raced back to the main
hall. As they ran through the different
zones they could see that things were
back to normal again: the model planes

were under control, the steam wheel was turning quickly and the space rocket was surrounded by hundreds of glowing stars. There was no sign of the goblins. The girls thought they must have gone back to the Ice Castle when they realised they had lost the goggles.

Kirsty reached stand 1D and quickly pulled on her lab coat and safety goggles.

Rachel stood at the front of the crowd to watch the Wetherbury High experiment.

It involved making multi-coloured bubbles in lots of different sizes. The bubbles floated and flew around the area like a magical moving rainbow!

Everything went perfectly and the audience cheered as Kirsty's school was awarded first place.

108

Rachel was pleased to see that the other schools, whose experiments went badly when Carly's goggles were with the goblin, had the chance to do them again and they all worked really well.

"What an exciting day!" said Kirsty a little later, as the two friends sat in the Science Museum's café, enjoying frothy hot chocolate with marshmallows.

"It was," agreed Rachel. "And the adventure isn't over yet. Tomorrow it's the school disco, and we still have one more magical object to find!"

109

The Dazzling Disco

Contents

Disco Countdown

"Phew! There's so much to do," said Rachel, looking at the huge pile of decorations in front of her.

"I know," replied Kirsty, untangling a long string of sparkly bunting. "But the hall will look great when it's decorated!"

The two friends were at Tippington School, starting to get things ready for the disco that evening. They had spent the last few days together, as their schools and two others were taking part in a competition, which had included a spelling bee and a science contest. Both events had almost been a disaster because Jack Frost and his goblins had stolen Carly the Schoolfriend Fairy's magical objects! But the girls and their fairy friend had outwitted the naughty creatures.

Now there was just one of Carly's objects left to find – the magical glitter ball. This made sure that all special school events, such as sports days and discos, went brilliantly.

"I wonder where everyone else is?" asked Rachel, looking at the clock on the hall wall. "We said we'd meet here at ten o'clock."

"How many of you are there on the organising committee?" wondered Kirsty, searching in the bag of decorations. "Oooh!" she cried, snatching her hand away from the bag.

"Are you all right?" asked Rachel.

"Something tickled my hand," said Kirsty, looking surprised.

All of a sudden the bunting whizzed up into the air. One of the triangles of material unfurled and a tiny fairy shot out!

"Hello, girls!" called Carly, shaking her wings and smoothing her dark hair. "I'm sorry, I didn't mean to scare you by appearing so suddenly."

"Hi, Carly," smiled Rachel. "It's lovely to see you again!"

"Thank you so much for helping me to get my bookbag and goggles back," said Carly, landing on Rachel's shoulder. "But I'm afraid that your disco tonight will go horribly wrong if we don't find my glitter ball soon!"

Suddenly, the friends heard an enormous crash, followed by loud howls. The noise startled Carly so much she shot back up into the air like a tiny firework!

"What is that racket?" cried Kirsty, covering her ears with her hands.

"I think it's coming from one of the music rooms," said Rachel. "Let's investigate!"

The three friends made their way towards the music department. As they approached the door to the practice room, the noise stopped and instead the girls heard familiar voices. Screeching and bragging...goblin voices!

Kirsty, Rachel and Carly peered into the room. The five missing members of the organising committee were sitting down on the floor, paying close attention to three goblins. The goblins were dressed in oversized T-shirts, baggy trousers and baseball caps. They were standing by a drum kit, and each was holding a microphone.

"Well, that explains the noise," muttered Carly crossly. "But I can't see my glitter ball."

"Let's listen in to find out if they give us any clues," said Kirsty.

"You see," they heard one of the goblins say, "as we've just demonstrated, we are *brilliant* musicians. We're going to play at your disco tonight!"

"Awesome!" laughed Phil, who was

in Rachel's class. "It's going to be great when you start at Tippington School!"

"What?" spluttered Rachel, as Kirsty quickly closed the door. "Why are the goblins coming to my school? And why don't the others notice how strange they look? Something funny is going on."

"Yes," frowned Carly. "My glitter ball must be nearby and its magical powers are making your friends think the goblins are just cool, funny kids. But I don't know why the goblins think they'll be coming to school here.

123

I'm going to go to Fairyland and see what I can find out. I'll be back soon!" Carly blew a kiss to the girls and disappeared in a sparkly whirl.

The door of the music room opened, and the boys and girls came out. "Oh, hello!" said one of the girls. "Sorry we're late. We're ready to help out now."

Kirsty and Rachel exchanged a glance. They really wanted to stay close to the goblins, but they had to get things ready for the disco that evening.

"OK," smiled Rachel. "Let's get decorating." Hunting for the glitter ball would have to wait until later!

Goblin Pupils

"Your dress is so pretty," said Rachel, smiling at Kirsty as she twirled in front of the mirror. "I love the sequins on it!"

"Thanks," said Kirsty. "Yours is lovely too, blue really suits you!"

It was teatime and the two friends were at Rachel's house, getting ready for the school disco. They had spent most of

127

the day at Tippington School, decorating
the hall and getting all the tables set
up for the party food and drink. It had
been hard work because, with Carly's
glitter ball missing, lots of the decorations
kept falling down or were mysteriously
broken. The girls and the rest of the
committee had done their best, but they
knew they had to get the glitter ball
back to Carly as soon as possible!

"I wonder what those sneaky goblins
were up to today,"
said Rachel,
fastening her
hair with a
glittery clip. "It
seems strange
that we didn't see
them all afternoon."

"We should head back to school soon," said Kirsty. "If we get there before everyone else hopefully we'll find the goblins *and* the glitter ball!"

The girls ran down to the kitchen to see what time they could get a lift to school. Both of Rachel's parents were making party food for the school disco. As Rachel pushed the kitchen door open, a cloud of smoke drifted out.

129

"Is everything OK?" coughed Kirsty. "What happened?"

"Oh dear, things aren't going well at all with the disco food!" said Mr Walker, wiping a smudge of flour from his nose. "Normally my cheese straws are delicious but this lot are horrid." He showed the two girls a tray full of blackened sticks.

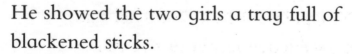

"My brownies aren't very tasty either," groaned Mrs Walker. "And they seem to have a strange tinge of green. Girls, do you want a lift to school soon? I think I'll drop you off and then come back here to try and sort out the food."

Kirsty suddenly spotted a flurry of sparkles in the corner of the kitchen. There was Carly, hiding behind a packet of flour!

She nudged Rachel, who moved closer to Carly so the pretty little fairy could flutter behind her hair.

"Yes, please, Mum," Rachel said. "Can we leave in about five minutes? We just need to get a few more things together for the disco."

The girls quickly ran back up the stairs to Rachel's room.

131

"Hi again, girls," said Carly. "I've had a *very* busy day in Fairyland, trying to find out what's going on and why Jack Frost wanted my magical objects. I'll create a Seeing Pool so I can show you what's been happening."

The little fairy fluttered up to Rachel's mirror and waved her wand. A rippling picture emerged.

The scene showed Jack Frost and his goblins in a classroom. Jack Frost seemed to be trying to teach the goblins maths. But the goblins used the pen and paper he had given them

to draw silly pictures of each other and
to make paper aeroplanes. The scene

faded, and Rachel and Kirsty saw Jack
Frost peeking into Carly's classroom in
Fairyland. Sitting at their desks were
lots of well-behaved fairy children, all
listening carefully to Carly's lesson.

"AHA! School is what my silly goblins need," cried Jack Frost. "I'll send them to a *proper* school in the human world. That will teach the goblins to respect authority and listen to ME! We'll steal the objects that belong to that silly fairy, so my goblins get a head start at school. Hee hee!"

With the sound of Jack Frost's icy chuckle ringing in everyone's ears, the Seeing Pool faded. Carly turned to the girls, her pretty face serious. "You

134

see, Jack Frost stole my magical objects to control the goblins. He thinks that sending them to school in the human world will make them better behaved."

Surprising Sounds

Rachel and Kirsty looked at each other in shock. "But...but the goblins can't go to school in our world," said Kirsty. "People will soon spot that they are anything but human!"

"You're right," said Rachel. "We must get the glitter ball back and make the goblins go home to the Ice Castle before they cause any more trouble."

The girls put their shoes and coats on, and waited in the hall for Mrs Walker. They felt a little sorry for Rachel's mum and dad – as long as the glitter ball was missing, all the food her parents made for the disco would taste awful!

Just a few minutes later, Kirsty and Rachel arrived at Tippington School, with Carly hiding in Rachel's bag. They made their way to the school hall, looking in each room to see if they could spot any goblin activity, but all was quiet. The disco wasn't due to start for another half an hour and there was nobody around.

The hall should have been beautiful after all the decorating, but instead it looked a bit of a mess. The bunting had fallen down and the helium balloons were on the floor.

"Let's see if the coloured disco lights work," said Kirsty, flicking the light switch. The lights came on and flashed prettily, sparkling against the disco balls that were hanging in front of the stage. Kirsty and Rachel smiled at each other happily. But then, one by one, the lights went out until just the green light remained on, casting a spooky green glow around the room.

Suddenly the girls heard a familiar icy voice coming from the side of the stage.

"Get out of my way. *I'm* the lead singer in this group and *I* need to check my vocals!" It was Jack Frost!

The three friends quickly ducked under the party food table. Then they peeked out and saw three goblins following Jack Frost. Each goblin was wearing a tight white catsuit, decorated with silver lightning bolts. Two goblins carried guitars and the third headed to the drum kit already on stage.

141

The Ice Lord was wearing a baggy white and silver onesie with a pair of huge silver high-top trainers that made him even taller than usual. Perched on his spindly nose was the biggest pair of sunglasses the girls had ever seen. And around his neck, worn as a pendant, was Carly's glitter ball!

"One two, one two!" called Jack Frost loudly into the microphone. He turned around to count the goblins in and then began to rap:

My name's Frosty and I'm the best,
I'm way cooler than all the rest!
My goblin crew is The Gobolicious Band,
Together we make the iciest sounds!

"Wow," cried Kirsty, looking surprised "they sound amazing!"

"That's the power of my glitter ball," said Carly sadly. "And they're going to use it to show off at the school disco!"

"Hmm," Rachel pondered. "I think I have an idea for how to get your glitter ball back. What does Jack Frost care about more than anything in the world?"

Kirsty thought for a moment. "Himself!" she cried.

"Exactly," smiled Rachel. "Let's use that to get the glitter ball from him!"

Glitter Ball Tricks!

The two girls and their little fairy friend bravely walked towards the big stage to speak to the Ice Lord.

"Jack Frost, please can we have a word with you?" Rachel called politely. Jack Frost peered down at the girls and Carly through his enormous sunglasses.

"What do you silly girls want?" he asked rudely.

"We just wondered, who will do the chores in the Ice Castle when all the goblins are at school in the human world?" asked Kirsty innocently.

The Ice Lord scowled crossly. "Pah! The lazy things will only be in school for a few hours each day, they'll have plenty of time to spend on me."

Rachel stepped forwards. "The thing is, after the goblins have finished their lessons, there'll be after-school activities, and lots of homework. There won't be much time for anything else."

"But who will serve me my yummy ice cream and massage my feet?" Jack Frost wondered.

Carly fluttered forwards to address the Ice Lord. "Why don't you let *me* teach the goblins? I can organise lessons at your Ice Castle. That way the goblins will have lots of time to help you. But I need *you* to return my glitter ball to me."

149

The girls exchanged a worried look. Would the Ice Lord be convinced?

Jack Frost narrowed his eyes. "I don't want them picking up even more bad habits! No, the goblins will be going to school here and that's the end of it. Now, get out of my way before I turn you all into icicles!"

The mean creature pointed his icy wand at the friends and they quickly ran down the stage.

"What do we do now?" cried Carly, her little wings drooping unhappily.

"It's time for action!" Kirsty said with a determined look on her face. "Carly, can you turn us into fairies? And would you be able to magic up one large glitter ball that's light enough for Rachel and me to carry? I've got an idea!"

"Of course!" said Carly, waving her wand. The girls felt themselves grow smaller and smaller. Shiny wings appeared on their backs and a sparkly giant glitter ball, as light as a feather, appeared in their hands!

151

Rachel and Kirsty flew back onto the stage, clutching the new giant glitter ball between them.

"Yoo hoo!" they called to Jack Frost. "We just came to say we don't need your glitter ball any more because we have this amazing new glitter ball!"

"A new, giant glitter ball?" exclaimed the Ice Lord, his eyes widening. "Look how big it is. Oh, I want it!"

"You can have this new, super-sparkly glitter ball," said Kirsty firmly, "as long as you return the one you have to Carly. It's hers and she needs it back."

Jack Frost wasn't too sure. He looked at Carly's glitter ball around his neck and suddenly realised how small it was. "Fine," he grumbled. "This one isn't big or glittery enough anyway!" and with that he took the glitter ball off.

"Now, Carly!" called Rachel, and Carly flew onto the stage and picked up her magical glitter ball. She hugged it tight and fluttered a happy loop-the-loop in the air!

"Here you go," said Kirsty, and the two friends handed over the giant glitter ball to Jack Frost.

"Wow!" he exclaimed, holding it up to the green lights, so that thousands of tiny light particles glistened on the stage. The goblins ran up to admire the new glitter ball and Jack Frost proudly showed it off to them.

"We did it!" cheered Rachel and Kirsty, giving Carly a huge hug. The three friends flew off the stage.

"Girls, you were amazing," cried Carly. "Now, I must take this back to Fairyland right away! Thank you for all your help." The little fairy quickly turned Rachel and Kirsty back into girls and then disappeared in a puff of fairy dust.

Jack Frost and his goblins headed off the stage. Jack Frost was holding the glitter ball and the goblins were jumping up and down trying to touch it.

Just then, the sound of excited voices came from the hall. The disco was about to begin!

A Magical, Musical Time

The girls quickly made their way into the hall. Now that Carly had her glitter ball back, everything looked amazing! The lights flashed with all the colours of the rainbow and the music sounded great. The party food on the table looked scrumptious and the ceiling was covered in lots of tiny glitter balls.

The girls were were just nibbling at some of Mr Walker's tasty cheese straws, when Kirsty saw something out of the corner of her eye.

"Pssst!" It was Carly, hovering behind a heart-shaped balloon, accompanied by her friend, Jade the Disco Fairy.

"Girls, I know you're having fun here, but will you come to Fairyland with us? We're having a magical disco and we'd love you to join us."

"Yes, please!" chorused the girls. They knew that time in the human world would stand still while they were away, so they would still be able to come back and enjoy the school disco!

Rachel and Kirsty slipped out of the hall and stood behind a rail of coats in the corridor. They held hands as the fairies waved their wands and they were caught up in a glittering whirlwind. They were off to Fairyland!

Just a few seconds later, the girls and their fairy friends landed in the Great Hall of the Fairyland Palace. Rachel and Kirsty had been in the hall before but they had never seen it looking so beautiful. The ceiling had been transformed into the night sky, with stars twinkling and shooting from one side to the other. The Twilight Fairies, who had

created the display, waved happily to the girls. Jade the Disco Fairy was joined by the other Dance Fairies, and in no time everyone was dancing to the brilliant music performed by the Music Fairies.

Queen Titania and King Oberon, the wise and kind rulers of Fairyland, came to greet the girls.

"Rachel and Kirsty, we wanted to give you a gift to say thank you for helping Carly," smiled Queen Titania. She took out two small boxes from the pocket of her robe and handed them to the girls. They gasped as they saw that each box contained a beautiful charm bracelet, complete with a glitter ball charm that sparkled under the night sky.

"Thank you so much, Your Majesties!" the girls cried, fastening the charm bracelets around their wrists.

"And now, we have a special musical surprise for you all," King Oberon called to the crowd. "Please join me in welcoming on stage Frosty and his Gobolicious Band!"

All the fairies looked surprised to see Jack Frost and his goblins as they came onto the stage, looking a bit uncomfortable. As the band started to warm up, the king put an arm around each of the girls.

165

"You see, girls, although Jack Frost shouldn't have taken Carly's objects, he did a good thing today by returning the glitter ball. And good acts should always be rewarded. Besides, he really is rather a good musician!" said the kind king with a twinkle in his eye.

The girls smiled and clapped as Jack
Frost and his goblins started to play.
In no time at all the Showtime Fairies
started dancing and Frosty's Gobolicious
Band looked on top of the world!

After chatting to their friends and enjoying some delicious fizzing strawberry sundaes, it was time for Rachel and Kirsty to return to their school disco.

Carly gave the girls a huge hug and with a wave of her wand the girls found themselves back at Tippington School.

Very soon it was time for the award ceremony, and Kirsty was delighted that Wetherbury High had won the best science experiment award for their bubble display!

"Wow, this has been such an exciting week," said Rachel as the two friends sat down in the hall, watching everyone have lots of fun.

"It's been amazing," smiled Kirsty, playing with her glitter ball charm. "I'm sad it's over but I'm sure we'll have more amazing adventures with our very special fairy friends!"

169

Now Kirsty and Rachel must help...

Mae the Panda Fairy

Read on for a sneak peek...

Kirsty Tate gazed happily at the tall hedgerows, her bare arm resting on the open window as the car travelled along the bumpy country road. Pretty red, yellow and pink flowers were tangled among the green leaves. She could smell the tang of cut grass and the earthiness of freshly turned soil.

"We're nearly there, girls," said Mrs Tate from the driver's seat. "Look!"

She slowed the car and pointed to a signpost at the side of the winding road. WILD WOODS NATURE RESERVE 2 MILES

Kirsty smiled at her best friend Rachel Walker, who was sitting beside her.

"I'm so excited," said Rachel. "The sun's shining, we've got all of the summer holidays stretching ahead of us, and a whole week to spend here with the animals."

It was the start of the summer holidays, and Kirsty and Rachel were on their way to Wild Woods, the local nature reserve. Rachel was staying with Kirsty, and their parents had arranged for them to spend every day that week there as volunteers. As the car turned up a rough, narrow track, their hearts were racing with anticipation.

"It's going to be amazing to be helping out as junior rangers," said Kirsty. "I can't wait to see the animals!"

At the end of the track was an archway, printed with green words:

WELCOME TO WILD WOODS
NATURE RESERVE

Mrs Tate drove through the archway and stopped the car next to a small wooden hut. The door of the hut opened and a tanned, dark-haired woman came out. She was wearing khaki shorts, a white shirt and walking boots, and she smiled and waved at them.

"Look, there's Becky," said Mrs Tate. "She's the head of Wild Woods."

Rachel and Kirsty jumped out of the car and Becky walked over to them.

"It's great to meet you both," said Becky, shaking their hands and smiling. "I'm really pleased that you're going to be spending this week with us. It's great to meet young people who are interested in conservation."

"We can't wait to get started!" said Rachel exitedly.

"I thought you should begin by going off on your own to explore the reserve," said Becky. "It's the best way to get a feel for it. I'll meet you back here this afternoon and give you your first task."

"That sounds like great fun!" chorused Kirsty and Rachel.

Read **Mae the Panda Fairy** to find out what adventures are in store for Kirsty and Rachel!

STAGE COACH

Learn to Sing, Dance and Act with
Stagecoach Theatre Arts Schools
For young people aged 4-18 years

600 schools nationwide!
Find your nearest school at:

Wow your
friends with...

Par@ties
Stagecoach

www.stagecoach.co.uk

RAINBOW magic™

Competition!

Three Stagecoach parties to be won!

To celebrate the release of Carly the Schoolfriend Fairy
we have three amazing Stagecoach parties to give away!

Two party hosts in full costume will entertain you
and your friends for up to two hours of party fun!
And if that wasn't enough, each party guest will receive a balloon,
party prize and stickers, as well as a Rainbow Magic book to take
home after the fun and magical event!

To be in with a chance of winning all you have to do is send
us a letter! Tell us why you love Rainbow Magic books and why
you think you should be the lucky winner of a Stagecoach party
for all your friends!

Once you've finished your entry all you have to do is send it to:
Rainbow Magic, Carly the Schoolfriend Fairy Competition,
Orchard Books, 338 Euston Road, London, NW1 3BH

Competition open only to UK and Republic of Ireland residents. No purchase required.
One prize draw will take place on 3rd February 2014.
Only one entry per child.
For full terms and conditions please see www.hachettechildrens.co.uk.

Robyn the Christmas Party Fairy

Join Kirsty and Rachel as they meet
a brand-new Rainbow Magic friend!

www.rainbowmagicbooks.co.uk